Max jumped around his room. He couldn't keep still. Today he and Old Ted were going to his Grandpa's house for his first ever sleepover. He was so excited.

Grandpa cooked a special dinner for Max;
it had all his favourite foods.
He was even allowed three scoops
of chocolate ice-cream for dessert.

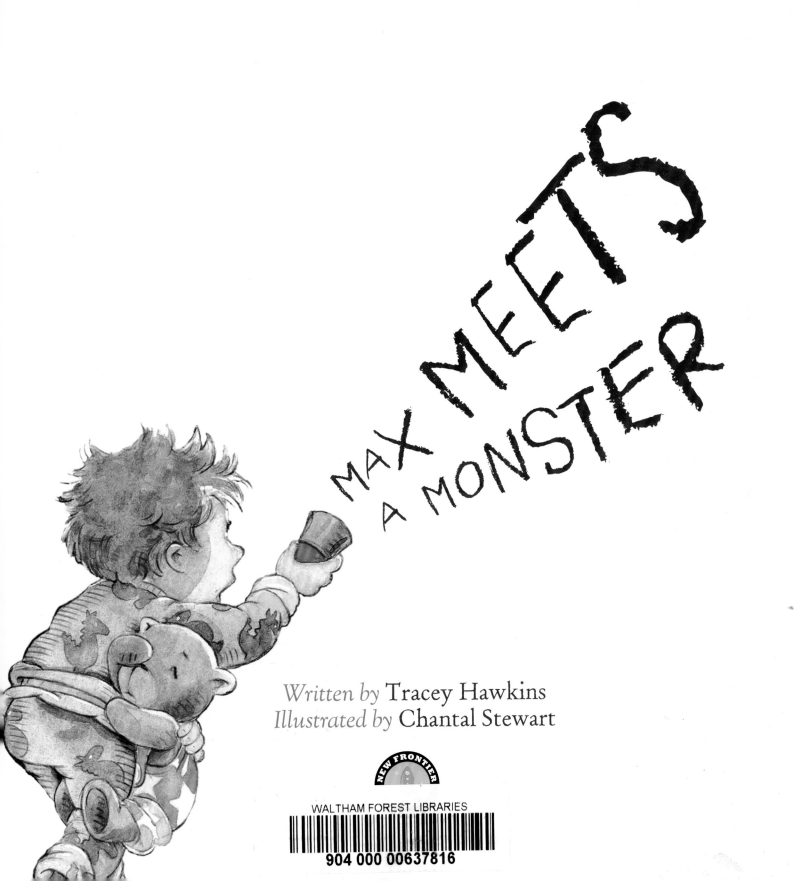

MAX MEETS A MONSTER

Written by Tracey Hawkins
Illustrated by Chantal Stewart

To Sarah, Samuel and Julian . . .
for believing in me.
TH

To Claire Madeleine and her Monsters.
CS

After dinner Grandpa and Max played with lots of very old small toy cars.

They had belonged to Max's father when he was a little boy.

When it was time for bed, Max put his torch next to
his pillow, snuggled up to Old Ted,
and drifted off to sleep.

Eeeemmmmppppphhhg Snarg Snaghhmph.

Max woke with a start.

A snorting, snuffling sound echoed around his room.

Max lay very still, his eyes wide open with fright.

Eeeemmmmppppphhhh. Snaarrgghhh, went the noise.

What could make such a horrible sound?

Was it something under his bed?

Could it be a monster making all that noise?
Max grabbed his torch, leaned over the side of his
bed and quickly turned on his torch.
No monster there.
Only a pair of Grandpa's old boots.

The noise grew louder. Max's heart thumped harder.
K thump, K thump, K thump. Eeemmmpppphhhgh.
The spluttering, snorting sound was coming from
outside the room.

Max
picked up
his torch
and Old Ted;
Max knew Old
Ted might get
scared if he was left
behind.

Together they tiptoed out
of the room in search of a
monster.

Max shone his torch around the walls; no monster there.

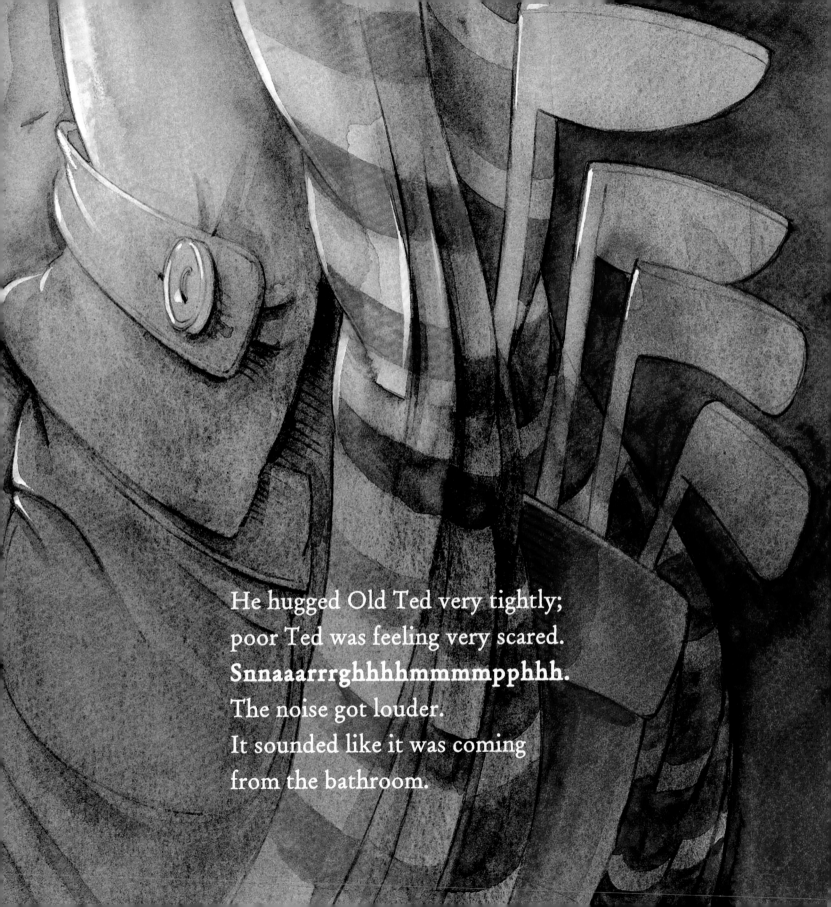

He hugged Old Ted very tightly;
poor Ted was feeling very scared.
Snnaaarrrghhhhmmmmpphhh.
The noise got louder.
It sounded like it was coming
from the bathroom.

Could a monster be in the bathroom? Max slowly slid open the bathroom door …

He quickly turned on the light. The bathroom was empty.
No monster there.

Snnnaa

The grunting grew louder. It was very close.
Eeeeeaaaaaaggghhhrrrgghhhmmhm.
Max crawled along the floor, dragging
Old Ted behind him.

The torch wobbled in his hand
making scary shadows on the walls.
Slithering like a snake Max and
Old Ted slid into the living room.
Eeeeemmmmgggghhhpppgh.
The noise was getting louder.
And louder.
Eeeeeaaaarrrrgggghhhh

Thumpty, thumpty, thumpty
went Max's heart.
The monster was here.
Eeemmmmgggggrrrraarrghpmm,
Snnnaarrgghhssnnaargh.
Awful snorting sounds
were coming from the
big brown couch.
Max was getting closer
to the monster.

Carefully and quietly he climbed to the top of the couch.

Shaking with fear he shone his torch.

Max could see the monster's mouth opening and closing.

Suddenly the torch
slipped out of Max's hand.
It hit the monster on the
head with a loud thud.
'Aaaaaaarrrrgghhhh!'
bellowed the monster.

'**Aaaaaarrrrghh,**' screamed Max as he fell
off the top of the couch, landing
right on top of the monster.

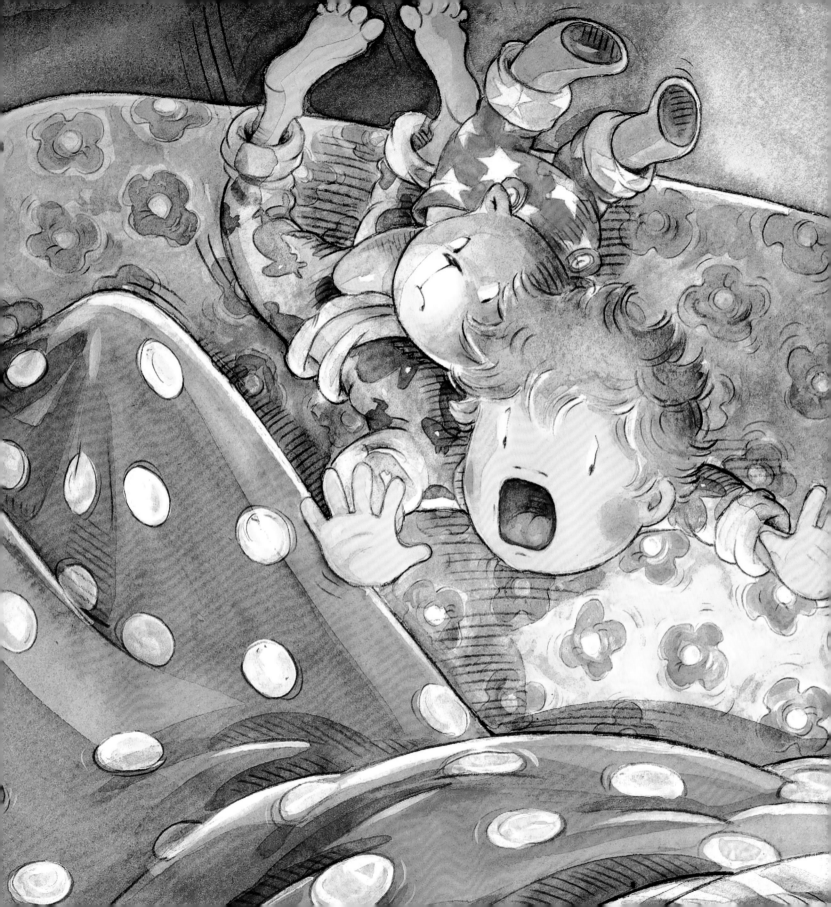

'**Uugh**,' groaned the monster.
'Grandpa?' said Max.
'Is that you Max?' said Grandpa.
'I thought you were a monster,'
sighed Max.
'A monster with a bump on his head,'
said Grandpa rubbing his head.

Max laughed and gave his Grandpa a big monstrous hug.